Published by Ad Hoc Fiction.
www.AdHocFiction.com

Purchasing Information:
Paperback available from www.AdHocFiction.com
E-book available from all usual outlets.

Printed in the United Kingdom.
First Printing 2023.

ISBN paperback 978-1-915247-48-3
ISBN e-Book 978-1-915247-49-0

A Learning Curve

by

Jan Kaneen

AdHoc Fiction

To my sons, Bob, George and Harry – the best teachers in the universe.

Contents

1) Prologue

Recipe for Disaster 1969

Ingredients

- 1 small child (aged 4 is best)
- 1 tender parent completely out of their psychological depth
- 1 unexpected death – an accident or lethal illness will do – a pulmonary embolism is ideal
- Lashings of raw grief
- Packets of emotional naivety
- A dash of collusive silence lightly tossed in a dressing of complete and utter denial

Method

- Following unexpected loss of parent, surviving parent should reduce/cure grief by
- re-marrying as soon as possible
- New family unit should re-hash dead parent's passing

- After short resting period, existence of dead parent should be reconstituted
- Photos of dead parent should be burned and mentions of them pared from familial narrative
- Reasons should be cooked up as to why step-parent must be called Mum/Dad
- Clarify to child that new narrative is what really happened, roasting, reducing, sweetening and/or coddling as appropriate
- Leave to simmer

2) Event Horizons

The black hole shifts; it's been getting darker with every chew of cornflakes. When it's become so dark it's absorbed every last bit of light in the known universe, it's a toxic concentration of negative energy. It hates her, hates this house, hates this filthy little planet.

But most of all, it hates her.

The black hole rages out, storming through time and space for the ten minutes it takes to get to the bus stop where it waits in the rain until the bus pulls up, at which point it gravitates upstairs. Once there, it settles itself down on the usual seat that's always saved by best mate Sheila and spews out dark matter all the way to school.

By the time the bus pulls up outside the sprawling concrete comprehensive, the black hole feels a little less intense, and by morning registration has even started to perceive the possibility of other realities beyond the fringe of its distortion field. Midway through double physics when Dr Sharples starts banging on about Aristotle's vacuum and different sorts of infinity, it disperses in a puff of super-focused concentration, and Sharon's able to think clearly again – not about the woman she's called mother for the last twelve years but about the lesson she's being taught. When the bell rings and breaks her focus, an image of her stepmother sneaks into her mind – a stooped little figure leaning over the kitchen table taking a damp cloth to all the hard surfaces, wiping away the lies from Formica and pine where they've left a greasy deep-fat film. Sharon feels a flash of sadness cascading through her. It's a deep sadness but also fleeting because it always morphs into hollow anger that always drags the blackness back. She dispels the image of her stepmother and chucks her exercise book into her satchel, stalks off to double maths with her head held high, full of unshakeable, unswerving certainty that no one will ever be able to distort the truth or wipe away her version of events, not in an infinity of forevers.

3) The Behaviour of Smoke

'Oi, Dilly Daydream, wake up, we're here,' chivvies Dad, jolting me out of my reverie. 'Here,' is Waverley Crematorium in Burnley and 'we' the short blonde Jacksons, all scrubbed up in our blackest Sunday best. It's December 1983 and I've come home a week early from the end of my first term studying physics at Aberystwyth Uni to say goodbye to Grandad Frank. We climb out of the shiny black funeral car and the afternoon air is icy, the sky wintery pink. We assemble with the other mourners, nodding sombre hellos, then go in two by two following the pallbearers into a high-ceilinged room. A long, thin carpet runs down the middle and, either side, rows of benches radiate out like ribs. They slide Granddad Frank onto a platform at the front as a faceless officiate calls him Francis, a name none of his friends ever used. We sing 'Amazing Grace' or 'Jerusalem'; I don't remember which. The eulogy makes strangers of both my dead grandparents so I give up listening and let my mind slip back to dilly-daydream-land where I think about lads I might shag when I get back to Aber; names I might call my children one day; if Grandad's body will be carbonised into mostly gaseous or solid material.

Afterwards, I slope off round the back for a private cry and consolatory fag. Curls of grey smoke rise from the redbrick crematorium chimney, getting lighter the higher they rise, dissolving into nothing in the pearly pink December sky. I take a long-hard drag, and push a cold, left hand deep into my coat pocket. An arm slips through the crook of mine. It's my kid brother. I catch the mischief in his eyes.

He nods upward and says in a Lancashire twang much broader than his usual accent, 'Ey up our Sharon, theer I go in a puff o' smoke.'

He's such a good mimic is our Alan – he's got Grandad down to a T. We shake, laughing as quietly as we can, but it's impossible.

I'm just about to say, shush you idiot, Dad'll hear, when Dad appears from nowhere.

'For crying out loud, you two, show some bloody respect,' he hisses, then walks away too sharply. You can tell from the back of his head he's furious.

I take a casual drag and say, 'Come on, Our Kid, we'd best be getting back. He'll burst a blood vessel if we keep the funeral car waiting, and your mother'll be none too pleased neither.'

A frostbitten wind whips up the leaves as his face drains of laughter.

'*Our* mother,' he says.

I take a cold-sharp breath, but the wintery air does nothing to cool the white-hot surge flaring through me. I jerk my arm from his, throw the fag onto the floor, twisting my foot so the glowing tobacco turns grey on the pavement. I march to the car without looking back.

Granny and Grandad are yesterday's smoke so there's nothing binding me to these deluded losers any more. When I go back to Aber after the holiday, that'll be that – bridges torched, carbonised, cremated. I will not be coming back.

4) What Went Through My Mind in the Lecture About the Butterfly Effect in Chaos Theory – the Phenomenon Whereby a Minute Localised Change in a Complex System can have Large Effects Elsewhere

What if the lady at reception hadn't been the White Witch from Narnia, and reception hadn't been made of dark secret panels and a spidery staircase? What if the waiting room hadn't smelt of Dettol and goblins and been full of pale-faced ghosts coughing and wheezing and straining for breath? What if time hadn't stretched, making seconds into forever like it does when you're four-and-three-quarters, or there'd been music playing – something by The Beatles or

The Seekers so I couldn't hear the magazine pages rattling brittle as bony fingers turned them over and over and over? What if I hadn't jittered nearly out of my skin when the white-witch-lady called out my mum's name?

What if Dr Young had been smiley-faced with a kind-warm voice like Grandad Frank and not an ancient ogre with slicked-back silvery hair? What if he hadn't peered out from behind his troll-bridge desk and asked in exactly the same voice as the Child Catcher, if I was the sort of nice little girl that liked sweeties? What if I'd shaken my head as Mum went behind the screen, instead of sitting there on the too-big chair letting him press six Smarties into my hot little hand?

What if there'd been a bin or a purse or a pocket to put them in so the candy colours hadn't run into a sickly rainbow when he followed my mum behind the screen? What if their voices hadn't talked in magical spells as the Smarties melted into a sticky goo, and I hadn't pulled my hand up into the sleeve of my coat as Mum came out still tucking that long cotton shirt into her baggy black slacks? What if Dr Young hadn't bent down to whisper at the surgery door with breath that smelled of Uncle Joe's Mint Balls, now you will be a good little girl for your granny won't you, whilst your mummy's in hospital?

What if I'd raged and wailed and writhed and bitten and scratched and thrashed and spat and screamed, I won't be good, I'll never be good, then my mum'll stay at home with me where she'll be safe from goblins and monsters and you?

What if I hadn't just nodded my head and walked toward the stained-glass panes in the grand front doors that led out onto the busy main road, and Mum hadn't reached down to take my hand and shaken her head as she took out a starched white hanky from her big brown handbag and wiped my fingers clean with spit and smiles? What if she hadn't lifted me into the passenger seat of our blue Ford Anglia and driven us off into the same old future, raising a protective hand in front of me every time we stopped at traffic lights and junctions as if she knew something bad was going to happen, as if she knew what was coming?

5) What Went Through My Mind in a Tutorial About the Many-worlds Scenario – a Core Proposition of Quantum Theory where 'Reality' (the photons that produce the light-illusion we all occupy) Exists in Infinite Possible States until the Moment we Observe it, at which Point all Potential Versions Collapse into One Single Option

6) Equation for Change

2 × 3rd-year physics undergrads + 3 bottles cheap red wine + 1 dodgy condom ÷ the unshakeable constant that having a baby might resolve my childhood trauma = (a seriously imperfect) 2.5

7) Things I Saw and Felt Whilst Balancing a Tower of Pebbles on Aberystwyth Beach the Day I Finished my Finals

1. Cerulean sky, thistledown clouds, Steve playing chicken like a child in the waves.
2. Contentment as I searched for colour-matched pebbles – speckled ambers, rusty corals, warm apricots flecked with cream.
3. The baby whale inside me spinning somersaults as I positioned the final plum of weathered pumice.
4. Infuriation as the cairn toppled.
5. Realisation that I should've chosen pebbles for their potential to stay put as much as for their gorgeousness.
6. A flash of fear – maybe I should've used similar criteria selecting my baby's father.

7. Steve's caramel skin and sea-salt hair.
8. Decidedly unscientific certainty.

8) The Difference between Theory and Practice – an introduction

Postpartum psychosis is a rare mental health condition that affects one or two in every 1,000 new mothers. Research suggests it is an overt presentation of bipolar disorder that coincides with hormonal shifts soon after delivery. Onset can be sudden and usually occurs 7–14 days after birth.

'We can't keep calling him Baby, can we?' snaps Steve, plonking down a cup of tea on the bedside table.

I've just finished the last bite of jammy toast and am licking my sticky fingers.

'No,' I whisper, so as not to wake the baby.

'We'll decide tonight, then, as his one-week birthday present.'

Steve's words are a distant thrum.

My gaze, like yesterday and the day before, draws itself back to the baby. I brush his cheek with the tip of my middle finger, watching his eyelids. They're translucent like mother-of-pearl, flickering with what I take to be his dreams. My mind is dull with love.

'Do you hear me?' says Steve.

I nod without looking up as he walks to the bedroom door.

'And don't forget you've left the bath running.' His words seem faraway, quieter than my thoughts and take forever to ripple through the heavy hush.

When the door closes after him, I murmur, 'I won't,' then gaze at the baby, watch his white towelling Babygro rise and fall. Eventually I haul myself up, sliding my arm out slowly so as not to move him awake, then make a barrier of pillows to stop him rolling off the bed.

Symptoms often cascade rapidly and may include sufferers harbouring odd beliefs, like their baby is something to do with God, or The Devil.

Next door in the white-wooden bathroom I turn off the tap and get undressed, then sink into the milky water. I let names float around my head, each foretelling different futures. Jimmy will be a writer. Dylan will have his own bakery in the Gothic quarter in Barcelona, Albert will be a scientist who'll lead the research team that'll eradicate cancer. But an upstart thought cuts through the treacle. *How will you leave him when you start your teacher training? Only six weeks to go – the clock's tick-tick-ticking.* The irritating niggle's been nagging for days and I'm annoyed with myself for letting it spoil my morning. I get rid by standing up and focusing on the here and now, looking through the steam at my hazy reflection in the cabinet mirror, shrimp pink with pendant breasts hanging heavy, full again already, aching fuller still, leaking at the thought of him. I step out and dry myself, letting versions of the name roll around my mind, Albert Jackson, Alby Jackson, Bertie Jackson – imagining my saviour baby, all grown up, healing the world.

9) Unpunctuated Osmium

strangers passing so close outside I can smell their fag smoke and diesel fumes too from the lorries rattling past on North Parade that make the foundations shake and I can't believe I used to feel safe in here or took comfort from the outside being so close to the inside because there's only two flimsy inches of brick between me and it and a front door that opens out onto a thin pavement and if I could escape I would escape but I can't move because I'm made from the heaviest material known to humanity that I used to know the name of before I started changing and that I'd look up now if only I could lift my fingers because when you left us and went back to your parents' in Leamington Spa you said it was all bollocks and that the real truth is I'm a lazy bag of crap who should pull myself together and think about someone else for a change like the starving millions who'd give their right eyes to have half of what I've got and I know you're right I know you're right I know you're right but knowing it only makes me heavier still and I am telling the truth I really am telling the truth and I might not know the name of the heaviest substance known to humanity any more but things don't need to have names for them to be real and you said it yourself I'm like a huge black hole that drags everyone down exuding magnetic self-indulgence that seeps into everything around me and that I never lift a finger to help myself or anyone else for that matter but that's because I can't lift a finger because I'm too heavy to move anything more substantial than air or the oxygen inside the air and I'm struggling really struggling even with that

10)Paradoxical Voices as Evoked by Doors

a. **In a good moment:** portals, ways out. Clear escape routes. Full of potential. Moving forward. Moving through. Ways in too maybe. Thresholds into something new and better.

b. **In a bad moment:** barriers, locked, blocking, can't see through, blind traps, prisons, keep out, turn back.

c. **In a really bad moment:** pale ghosts. Hollow fingers tap-tap-tapping. *Don't touch the handle.* And threads of terror unravelling from my fingertips pulling me forward. *Don't touch the handle.* And twisted whispers reeling me nearer, winding me nearer... *don't touch the handle...* into the savage heart of whatever's waiting on the... *DON'T. GO. IN.*

11) Indisputable Proof of Parallel Universes

Years later, Bryn will say that the energy in Dr Hugh's waiting room changed the moment I opened the door. That when I stepped inside, a bolt of something like static electricity sparked through him. He flashed me a stunned grin, but I didn't smile back, apparently. I sat on a moulded plastic chair and stared straight through him, patting the back of the red baby sling strapped tightly over my donkey jacket.

'I'm not being funny,' he'll say in that sing-song Cambrian lilt of his. 'I mean, time didn't stand still exactly, but it did stutter a bit. You were sort of detached and dreamy, like you were under water or far away.' And he'll smile as he remembers, looking into the space between us like he's watching the ghosts of us live it again. 'There you were, sitting, with your blonde bob all frizzed up on one side like you hadn't brushed it when you got out of bed.'

And as he speaks, I'll follow his gaze, hoping to catch a glimpse of an echo of what he's re-seeing.

'It's so clear, so raw, like it's still happening,' he'll say, 'The smell of old magazines and wintergreen, and you sitting there sandwiched between Esme Jones and some snotty-nosed teenager coughing and sniffling and waiting his turn. Not the most romantic way to meet the love of your life, eh, cariad?' And when he says, 'love of your life', he'll switch his gaze to look deep inside me, not *at* my eyes but past and beyond them, his own grey gaze burning silver. 'It was the strangest feeling in all my life,' he'll say. 'A sort of drawing, moving, floating forward; like something was pulling and pushing me at the same time.'

And when he says these things, which he sometimes will, I'll smile and nod like I'm remembering too, but I won't say anything because, for me, it didn't happen. I don't mean it didn't happen *like that* – like I remember generally but disagree with the finer details, as people will when they share experiences from slightly different perspectives. No. My reality isn't the same but different; it's nothing – a void or vacuum that happened somewhere beyond my field of perception in a time when only me and Baby Albert existed. So, not wanting to sour his profound experience, I'll seem to agree, and over the years I'll reconstruct the moment from what he says so my tacit assent becomes less of a lie – being the only version of events I have. But my real truth is that Bryn didn't exist for a couple of weeks after that let's-call-it 'first meeting' – not until after the first batch of medication kicked in.

12) Different States of Broken

I stand still and naked on the faux fur rug in front of the two-bar electric fire.

'Don't move,' Bryn had said before dashing out. 'Don't move an inch.'

A silent tear runs down my hot cheek as I look at the scattered clothes and shards of broken pot lying round me, some pinprick sharp. Without moving, I see bigger pieces further away on the dark floorboards, arcs of broken bone china lying where they fell. I raise my gaze up past the glowing electric bars, to where it used to stand. Its mirror image stands there still, guarding the other end of the wooden mantelpiece, a round-backed spaniel with cavalier ears looking past me with glazed eyes. Grandad Frank's last gift to me.

The one that's left is already heavily mended. Spidery lines crackle across its opalescence where Superglue holds it together. I wince, motionless, as fragments of memory crash back from that time, sharp fragments, *stupid bitch*, cruel fragments, *cheap tatt*, hard fragments, *ugly piece of nothing*, go on then, pick it up.

But that was months ago, before Bryn, when I myself was badly broken.

Bryn comes back in, as naked as me except for his fireman's helmet, carrying a dustpan and brush.

'Stay still,' he says, bending at my feet to sweep the floor, patting flat-handed for pieces he's missed. 'I think we're okay.'

He fingertips the biggest pieces as fragments of earlier replay themselves in my mind, warm fragments, *love you, cariad*, breathless fragments, *love you too*, ecstatic fragments, *please don't stop*. I'd clung to the wall before my steadying palm had reached too far and tipped it over.

'It's not that bad,' he says. 'I think it'll mend, and when it does it'll match the other.' He kisses my forehead, then picks up two pieces and pushes them together. They slot into one another perfectly.

13) Cost of the Whirlwind

Item	Amount
2 last-minute budget flights	£498
Cheapo motel package	£500
Adding Albert to my passport	£5
Limo and dress hire	$300
Best man Babygro	£10
Elvis singing	$30
Marriage	$57
Pastor at The Little White Chapel Drive-thru	free with a $30 tip
Photographer/photos	$50
All-you-can-eat drive-through	$40
The look on our faces in the photo we'll keep on the dark-oak sideboard for as long as we both shall live	priceless

14) Waves of Change

Grey sky, grey road, grey rain; it's pouring down old women and sticks, not weedy English cats and dogs but proper mid-Wales, Cymraeg rain. Driving back from Bronglais Hospital in a swirling daze of whirling grey, washing along through murk and mist, floating, ghosting, shifting different. Penglais Hill's like liquid flint, the roofs, the sky reflected back. Swilling right then right again, climbing tight up Brynymor Road. Parking on our patch of tarmac just outside our brand-new home. Taking the photo from my handbag, heartbeat quick as the battering rain. Shiny paper between my fingers, silk-soft shiny between my fingers, and there it is in black-and-white. Charcoal background. Chalky waves. Bone-grey smears of brand-new life.

15) Forever Look

He stares through the cross-wired window, watching her as she sits propped up in the third bed along. She's crooning to the waffle-blanket bundle in the crook of her left arm. Suddenly, he feels uncomfortable, like a peeping Tom, and switches focus to catch his own grey ghost in the silvery glass – dog-tired, stubbly cheeks, anxious face still smudged with smoke. He swings the ward door open, wishing he'd had time to have a shower as mingled scents of starched sheet and new-born baby pull him forward. He feels her look up but concentrates on the tight line that is her mouth, his heart throbbing in his throat because he's certain his explanations will mean nothing, but what could he do? Everything happened so fast and three weeks early, and he was on the night shift attending a level one blaze in a field near Borth.

He musters his courage and raises his gaze. The look she shoots him comes from somewhere new, somewhere deep behind her shining eyes, and it changes everything. It lets him in. From that moment, whenever they clash or she's being smart-arse impossible, he'll remember that look and it will save them. And even when, in the coming storm, grief and darkness threaten to swallow them whole, he'll summon that look and it will be his beacon. And right at the end when there's nothing left, only longing and loss of everyone he cares for, that conjured look will burn as bright and potent as the first time he saw it, bringing courage and peace and something like hope, even as he takes his final breath.

16) The Difference Between Theory and Practice, 1

Symptoms of postpartum psychosis often include a combination of manic or depressive behaviours, such as hearing voices or seeing things that aren't there (hallucinations), and believing things that are not based on reality (delusions).

I climb out of the shower and grab the old cotton towel that's warming over the radiator and start to rub myself dry. The towel snags on something high up on the back of my leg. I try to tug it free, and a thread pulls loose. I'm surprised. There's nothing sharp about me, not any more. I run a hand into the puckered arc of my buttock and thigh, feeling for – well, I'm not sure what I'm feeling for – dry skin, perhaps, or maybe a splinter. My finger recoils and I see a garnet of blood forming cabochon on my fingertip. I lick it away then rifle round in the wicker drawer under the sink to find my compact mirror. I need to see what has made me bleed.

The tiny reflection is difficult to catch in the harsh white light. I twist to get into the right position. It casts no shadow and traps no colour, but, narrowing my eyes into slits and poking out my tongue, as though that will help, I just about see it. Growing out of my curds-and-whey skin is a thorn of glass – almost invisible, sharp and see-through.

'Get rid of it,' spits a rogue thought.

I do as I'm told, pulling hard, but it's impossible. It isn't on the outside stabbing in; it's on the inside stabbing out.

'Snap it off,' barks the alien thought.

I hold my breath and try, but a fractal of pain, lightening hot, stops me. I try again and again but I can't, even when I bite my lip to trick the pain.

Symptoms of postpartum psychosis may include panic, confusion and racing thoughts.

I scrabble round in the second drawer down. I might not be able to pull the thorn out, but I can make it disappear. Nail file in hand, I balance on the edge of the roll-top bath to reach underneath my leg, feeling my way, pressing gingerly into the skin until my fingertips reach the thick base of it. I run an exploratory rasp over the point. It's painless – like filing nails. I file and file, shearing it away into sparkles that fairy-dust the floor. It takes forever and when

I'm done, though the thorn isn't gone completely, it is blunted. I rub oil into the raw skin around it, then all over to soften myself back to normal, soft enough to hold my baby.

The baby!

I run naked into the bedroom. Baby Owain's sleeping exactly as I left him in his cot. I do what I've done so many times over the last few days and sleepless nights – I reach out to touch him, extending my finger to check he's breathing.

I only see it because the overhead light isn't on. The frail lamplight casts a shadow at exactly the right moment just before it connects. In the place where my mother's touch should be is a talon of glass, almost invisible, poised to slice. I freeze, then focus, seeing it clearly now – thicker at the bottom than the top, slightly hooked, tapering to a point. I scream.

It wakes him up. He starts to cry.

Common symptoms of postpartum psychosis also include paranoia and feeling useless as a mother.

I want to pick him up to soothe him calm. I need to feed him quiet to release the pressure in my breasts that nursing him will ease.

'Don't touch him,' spits the alien thought. 'You'll hurt him, with your thorns of glass.' So instead, I look down at his jerky kicks and desperate fists as he cries himself crimson.

'Thorns lead to more thorns,' growls the alien.

I turn my hands over, and sure enough, another crystal pinprick is almost breaking the surface of my right palm.

'There might be one on your breast.' The alien thought whispers my darkest fears like they're delicious. 'There might be one on your nipple.'

I blink away the image that springs into my mind, my insides shrivelling to nothing. Owain turns his head sideways, rooting, frantic to latch on. I hold him away from me, folding the thorn into the palm of my hand, feeling with my safe middle finger. The nipple is safe. I sigh with relief as his hard gums clamp down and we connect, then sit rigid against the wooden headboard, too afraid to move myself comfortable, trapped and stiff with a growing thirst. By the time he's finished and sleeping safely away from me in his cot, we're working out a plan, my alien and me.

17) The Quiet

It's in my dreams and deepest sleep, the tired alarm, then on the radio, in every slice of breakfast and the percolator's gurgle, in the doorbell and Jen's chatter when she calls to pick up Albert, in their footsteps down the path as I wave them off to nursery, in the quick-repeating wheels as I push the pram down to the seafront, in the little sea-salt pool in all the laughter and the splashing, in the babies and the mothers and the dark-brown swallowed coffee, in the constant background babble and the walk back up the hill, in the front door when it opens, in the front door when it closes, in baby Owain's breathing when he giggles, feeds and snuggles, in his shrieks and tired protests as I change his dirty nappy, in the engine when it starts, in the engine when it stops, in the thrum of passing traffic as I walk toward the shopfronts, in the bustle at the market and the jangle when I'm packing, in the spiteful nursery gate when it whinges shut behind me, in Albert's car-seat singing and the twisting of the door key, in Bryn's hello and in his kisses, in the dicing and the slicing, in the crunch and chomp of supper and the splatter of the bath, in the bear-hunt bedtime story and Albert's endless questions, in the sleep-tights and I-love-yous and the clicking of the switches, in the TV when it's on, in the TV when it's off, in every silence, every heartbeat, every breath – in *every* breath.

And because I'm ragged and I'm desperate for a single moment's quiet – I give in. And agree.

To do exactly what it tells me.

18) The Difference Between Theory and Practice, 2

As postpartum psychosis progresses, typically, it is a family member, often the partner, who realises something is wrong.

It's Saturday morning and I'm scrubbing hard, sterilising dozens of new bottles in my yellow kitchen gloves, screwing the brush round and round as hard as I can to scour the tainted plastic.

'Be seeing you then,' says Bryn from behind my back. I feel him hovering, wanting to kiss me goodbye.

'See you after your shift,' I say in monotone, screwing harder to avoid the kiss.

'Let him go,' yawns the alien. 'It's not like you can let him anywhere near you, is it?

Not with those disgusting claws.'

'S'pose not,' I reply, forgetting myself, too tired to argue.

'Did you say something?' says Bryn.

I turn and look at him like he's mad. He makes his face expressionless to hide what he's really thinking, then calls goodbye to Albert who's sitting in front of the TV, glued to his *Fireman Sam* video. Bryn walks over to the pastel carrycot, kisses his finger, and smears a dirty kiss onto Owain's sleepy cheek.

'Do you have to,' I say. 'The germs.'

'Bye,' he says, hesitating at the door.

I sit down at the table, seeing it all from far, far away.

'You'd better get a-filing,' singsongs the alien, 'so your claws are safe and short and secret.'

19) The Difference Between Theory and Practice, 3

It's rare for mothers with postpartum psychosis to harm their babies, but the cognitive disorganisation associated with the condition often results in them being neglectful of their baby's needs or harming themselves.

There's a noisy quiet echoing through the kitchen-diner in the wake of the slap. *Fireman Sam* has finished for the umpteenth time, and the blank TV screen is flickering black and blue as Albert stares at me from his beanbag. Baby Owain is wet faced, sitting in his bouncy chair. He's just stopped crying and is breathing in, in shocked, jerky sobs. I turn and stare at my naked hands in the washing-up bowl.

Owain was crying and I was so tired – I hadn't been keeping on top of things – I'd been letting myself go, letting my secrets show. Albert was whining at me to rewind his tape as I scrubbed and scrubbed at Owain's dummy. An unfiled talon, growing out of the end of my index finger, had pierced the marigold latex and let the dirty water in. I snapped the gloves off and hurled them wet against the wall, screaming wild and high like the banshee I am. They'd slapped hard as they hit, trailing a watery bruise down the magnolia paint.

'Chop it off,' snarls my alien. 'Chop it off, the whole bloody hand. Chop off the whole bloody useless thing,' and I watch as it claps its leathery hands, dances on its filthy feet, its glassy talons click-tapping on the Lino, so I don't hear Bryn behind me, home early from the station because he's worried sick and we really have to talk. I don't hear him reaching out to touch my shoulder. I swing round raising my claws ready to slash. He takes them in his hands, turning them over slowly. Time stops as he kisses my sharpest point, pressing his lip to its pinprick tip. I try to pull away and am surprised when it draws no blood.

That night, whilst the children sleep, I let him talk to my alien, and show him all my thorns.

20) Infinite Possibilities

Dear Editor,

In response to your Voices campaign, I'm writing to add my voice to the Recovery Chorus.

Eleven years ago, after the birth of my second son, I experienced terrifying delusions and hallucinations that I desperately tried to hide from everyone around me, but it was an impossible task and my husband soon realised something was terribly wrong. With me refusing to see a doctor and no idea what to do for the best, he contacted my family from whom I'd been estranged for several years. My birth mum died when I was four, but my stepmum, who'd been my mum's best friend, told him she'd helped my mum navigate the 'difficult' times after my own birth, and so understood the nature of the situation. My stepmum was a senior nursing sister in a large hospital in Burnley and she used her contacts to access outpatient treatment for me and I received better care than most could expect in 1989. Back then, postpartum psychosis (PP) was still medically undescribed, without recognised symptoms or treatment plans. In fact, writing this, I've set my experiences in the context of current clinical thinking for the first time, and been struck by what a textbook case I was. This feels normalising, therapeutic even and makes me appreciate how lucky I was getting the treatment I did. Sadly though, good treatment doesn't cure stigma, which is as real in 2000 as it was back then, a reason, I suppose, why mums like me don't talk about recovery. That's why I've gathered courage to write this after all these years, and because my life after PP has been really good. I'm a happily married part-time teacher with two fabulous sons who's had no recurrence of the symptoms, though, looking back, I think I had a misdiagnosed episode following the birth of my first son. For me, there have even been positive outcomes from having had PP. Growing up, I'd had a deeply troubled relationship with my stepmum who'd sort of airbrushed my birth mum out of existence, but the way she supported me through PP made her have to acknowledge the truth of her step-parenthood. This re-wrote our relationship and laid the worst of our demons to rest. I don't want to tempt fate because as a teacher of science and student of life, I know very well this is an infinite universe full of infinite possibilities, but having survived PP and having built a more honest relationship with my stepmum, I feel as qualified as I've ever been, to be able to cope with whatever trials and tribulations might lie ahead.

Sharon Jackson
Aberystwyth, Ceredigion

21) Impossibility

Sunlight trickles through the window onto the kitchen table, warm and golden like Tuesday's pancake syrup. She lays the breakfast things: two bowls, one red with guitars, the other blue with footballs, then two spoons that stand to attention by each. One says *Albert*, the other *Owain*. She sent off for them donkey's years ago, saving cardboard tokens from the sides of cereal packets, cutting them out carefully and keeping them in an envelope on the white-tiled windowsill above the sink. It took forever to collect enough to get both at once so they wouldn't fight over who got theirs first. She looks at the table and almost smiles. The daily ritual makes her feel nearly normal.

She's getting milk from the fridge when a lurch in the place her heart used to be tells her it's time. She glances sideways toward the stairs to make sure Albert hasn't seen, then dashes the blue setting away. It's safely back in the cupboard when he takes his usual place. She puts a mug of tea in front of him, dark brown with a dash of semi-skimmed. A bubble sails around the outside in the teaspoon's slipstream.

Albert smiles a watery orange squash sort of smile and says, 'You ok, Mum?' She smiles the same smile back. The air is thick with sunshine, claggy and heavy, so it's hard to breathe it in. He fills the bowl with cornflakes, reads through his homework as he eats. When the bowl is empty, he refills it and finishes a second helping, leaving a pinkish puddle in the bottom where the thin milk lets the red show through. He downs his lukewarm tea and goes upstairs to clean his teeth.

She washes up the bowl and the mug and puts them upside-down on the draining board. When he comes back, he's ready to go, in his reflective windcheater, with his S Club Seven rucksack on his back.

'Bye Mum,' he says, watching her closely as she tea-towels his bowl dry. 'Love you,' and he bends to kiss the top of her head like she used to do to him.

When he's gone, she sits in his seat and reverses time to see if she can bear it yet.

'But Hew Davis's is Swansea City,' cries Owain, 'and Dafid Jones's is Harry Potter.' His grey eyes well silver with disappointment. 'I'm never wearing it.'

'They must be richer than us then,' she snaps, still hurt by how upset he'd been. 'I work part time and your dad saves lives, not money.' Then more gently, 'We could customise it with stickers or stencils maybe.'

Back in the real world, her gaze fixes on the kitchen door and the black coat hook that always looks like a sideways question mark, and the plain cycle helmet still hanging there ugly as a horseshoe-crab, the colour of dirty sunshine, waiting for the impossible day she can bear to take it down.

22) How to Fill an Unfillable Void

1. Preheat oven to 180 degrees then go pick apples. In the wet's best, on the darkest day of autumn, when everything smells of mould and mushrooms and the garden looks like rust and cinders. But don't let the fruit ruin waiting for perfection.
2. Place apples in appropriate receptacle. I use a trug made from sheets of birch. It's got a long flat bottom, so the apples lie side-by-side without bruising when I hurry back inside to get out of the weather.
3. Wipe fruit carefully so skins shine like wintery cheeks, like Owain's used to when he came inside for a warm on snowy days when the stove was lit.
4. Don't peel. A little skin will give the edges a ruddy tinge, and anyway, it's good for you – full of roughage and it makes your hair curl – least that's what I always told Owain when he used to pull his face.
5. Slice into cored crescents that look like rose petals and place into buttered tart dish. I arrange

mine in circular swirls that coil inward and make a pattern that looks like forever.

6. Make caramel by heating butter and sugar. Some recipes say not to stir but I do because that's the bit Owain loved best – standing on his three-legged stool at the cooker in his Winnie-the-Pooh apron, watching the crystals dissolve into liquid gold.
7. Add five pinches of cinnamon. One for Mummy, one for Daddy, one for Albert and two for Owain, then a squeeze of lemon. An edge of sharpness is necessary to cut through the syrup. Pour over apples.
8. Take block of shop-bought pastry from fridge. This is a matter of preference, of course, so feel free to adapt to personal circumstance, but for me, time's way too short for homemade rough puff.
9. Roll thin and place on top of apples, tucking in edges like a child's blanket, then bake for fifty minutes.
10. As scent of caramelised apples creeps like yesterday into warm kitchen, pour glass of something lovely and remember – when you moved here to start again and planted the sapling what seems like a lifetime ago, when it meant nothing and you were so impossibly numb-and-sensitive-at-

the-same-time you couldn't feel anything though everything still managed to hurt – opening your eyes, birdsong, hearing your own name… and a year later when you finally scattered the ashes round the reedy stem… and the year after that, harvesting the first crop.

11. Smile or cry. It doesn't matter which.
12. Take tart from oven and cool, but not too much. Grief, hope, love, remembrance – all are dishes best served warm.
13. Eat as many slices as you need, savouring every last bitter-sweet mouthful until you're so tip-top full to the brim you think you'll never be able to manage another bite.
14. Take another bite.

23) Fixed

Why did Hitler hate gay people? Do fish know they're wet? Why is pink for girls?

Albert used to fill the drive back from rehearsals with questions and we'd talk all the way home. Now he flops into the car and stares out of the window and it's me that asks the questions.

Have a nice day, love?

So-so.

Shall we pop into the Spar?

Na.

Everything alright, love?

Fine.

I get clever and ask open questions that start with words like what or who, because they're harder to answer with single words and if I can get him talking again, I'll be able to read between the lines and deduce what's up.

What homework have you got?

Drama.

Who did you have lunch with?

No one.

What do you want for supper?

Shrug.

What's the bloody matter and how can I make it better?

That's what I really want to ask, but if I did, he'd clam up and shoot me that look, the one that's a mixture of scorn and leave-me-alone-for-pity's-sake.

I've deduced he's fallen out with Tudor Jenkins, but it can't just be that. I turn on Radio 4 to drown out my noisy thoughts but it doesn't work and I find myself analysing our conversations from when he was still communicating. We'd decided Hitler was a madman who hated everything he was and everything he wasn't, and that colour gendering's all in people's heads. We never did get to the bottom of fish and wetness though. I said fish probably know they're wet because they can feel it. He said I was judging things through the prism of my own experience and that fish have never been dry to compare their wetness to. I said that was a great point and that perhaps recognising wetness or dryness, or any other state of being, is made more apparent by comparative experience. He threw me a look. I was driving but I caught it out of the corner of my eye – a mixture of respect and maybe-you've got-something-there, Mother. But now, only days later, he's retreated completely and I'm analysing his silence like it's quantum theory.

I steer left onto the seafront as the frustration washes over me. Maybe it's the rising wind or the vast blackness of the waves beyond the white railings, but as I pull up outside home, the question explodes out of me.

He doesn't move.

I turn off the engine.

He sits still and quiet, staring forward as I breathe in the ozone tang of the hushing sea, remembering the day we moved here – a new start after what happened to Owain – a day when it never occurred to me that in an unimagined future, I'd be sitting in the car, waiting for my surviving child to share something terrible.

'Mum,' he says. 'I think I'm gay.'

The relief is exponential and before I have time to stop myself, the words have spooled out of my mouth. 'Is-that-all-I-thought-it-was-something-serious.' Then immediately I realise how awful that must sound.

'Do you want a hug?' I say, but he's already climbing out and my moment to say something wise and kind that'll stick with him forever has slipped from the missed-opportunity, ephemeral present into the fixed and rigid, unforgivable past.

24) Albert Defining Words Just Before I Challenge his Use of Possessive Pronouns

It's not been 'left'; it's deliberate. There's no point in 'making' something you're going to unmake the minute you use it. And you can't 'stain' black sheets. Black's an absence of colour – you can't 'stain' something that's not there. And 'caked-on's downright melodramatic. It's just a bit spattered that's all – dried-on at most. And mould's the opposite of 'filth' actually, especially on bread. In the olden days, they used to make it into moultices or poultices or something to treat infection. And anyway, Mother, you shouldn't even be in my bedroom, it's my space, my mould, my 'mess', not yours.

25) The Difference Between Schrödinger and Albert at Weekends

He slinks home at dawn, flowing past me, lithe and lean, sliding his twilight fur against my slipper socks. I put my mug down to scratch behind his ear, which he likes just long enough to tilt his head into the cup of my hand, but almost straight away he's had enough and springs up to the sink to steal a few cat-lick sips from the dripping tap. When he's drunk his fill, he lollops down, padding past with eyes fixed forward like there's no one here, then settles on the comfy sofa, curling into an immediate sleep. He's in exactly the same position when I come down from my shower, when I tidy the house, when I get home from the supermarket – but as I crash past, lugging bag after bag, eventually he wakes. Yawning in slow-motion, he casts me a slit-eyed glance, stretching everything until his claws peep out, then shadows past into the kitchen, skulking and hunkered like he's ready to pounce. His food bowl's empty, so he caterwauls until

I fetch his Felix, then purrs and circles as I fork it out. Once he's eaten, I don't exist, and he's barely aware of me as he grooms himself perfect. And when he leaves without a backward glance, all sleek and silky and twitching whiskers, I smile with pride as I watch him go, full of admiration at his independent sass. I say nothing about his standoffish attitude, or lack of gratitude, or how he treats this place like a bloody hotel. I don't screech, what did your last servant die of at the open front door as he disappears round the dark street corner. I don't whisper into the rolling sea-swell to be careful and sensible and home by midnight.

26) The Full 360 Degrees

'You're not normal, you know...'

I stare into my dressing-table mirror, patting splotches of moisturiser onto my cheeks.

'...you're mature or ageing...'

The new wrinkles round my eyes seem to deepen visibly as I ignore my stepmother.

'...you've really let yourself go recently.'

I don't react because she's been dead for eleven weeks and three days, but only physically; in every other respect, she's alive and well and living inside my head.

As a scientist, I know lots about thoughts and how they're connected by electrical impulses, so I presume she's in my synapses and neurons – a lurking electrical presence that no one else can hear.

'*The trouble with...*' she starts up, but I've had enough.

'Hush,' I snap, striding to the bathroom where I peer around the half-open door.

Albert's fingering super-firm, no-shine styling mud into his blond quiff.

'Nearly ready?' I ask.

He tweaks and teases without answering as the bathroom spotlights shine clear and white, revealing every speck of dust. My stepmother notices and tuts.

Albert has pongs and potions everywhere. Recently, his fragrance of choice has progressed from Lynx to a more sophisticated, later-teenage spray that smells quite nice.

'Like a tart's armpit,' sniffs my stepmother.

Five minutes later, I'm at the foot of the stairs bellowing, 'Get a lick on,' but Albert's listening to base-pumping hip-hop.

I race upstairs, shouting, 'Turn it down. You're going to miss your appointment at the bloody hairdresser's spending too long doing your...'

Albert mutes his iPod so when I bellow, 'bloody hair,' the quiet makes me sound unhinged.

He slopes past, shaking his perfectly coiffured head.

'Potty mouth,' barks my stepmother.

Outside, the undulating sea has an immediately restorative effect and, climbing into my Beetle, I aim a measured thought at my stepmother. *You had it easy with us before expensive haircuts and pricey phones became must-have teenage accoutrements*, then block out her forthright riposte by flicking on Radio 4.

Woman's Hour comes on, and before I have time to save myself, I've fallen into a long-gone Christmas, home from uni in 1983. Me and my stepmum are making trifle in the tiny scullery in Burnley for Grandad's wake, tippling cooking sherry at eleven-thirty a.m. 1983 Jenny Murray moves seamlessly from striking miners' wives to flapjacks as eighteen-year-old me says, 'Yuck – that's foul.'

'But you always loved it!' snorts my stepmother, looking hurt.

'Only because I didn't know any better.' The expression on my teenage face makes me wince.

Back in today, my stepmother says, 'This car's a skip on wheels. Look at all those

KitKat wrappers. No wonder you've piled on weight.'

I chuck the wrappers into my handbag as Albert hops into the passenger seat, his headphones plugged into his mobile phone. The car mumps into motion. By the time we park outside Curl Up and Dye, I'm in full flow.

'The trouble with teenagers nowadays is you're all obsessed with physical perfection.

See that tattoo parlour?'

Silence.

'Aw, leave him alone,' says my stepmother as Albert unplugs.

'See that tattoo parlour?' I repeat. His gaze follows my finger.

'That used to be a butcher, and that nail bar was Jones's Bakers.'

His face is blank as he says, 'And that tanning salon was the candlestick-makers, I suppose.' He swings outside, immediately adopting his outdoor street-swagger.

'Actually, it was a greengrocer's,' I call through the wound-down window, 'but candlestick-makers would do to make the point. The town centre used to sell *stuff*, like bread and meat, not services dedicated to…' I struggle to find the right word, then settle on preening. 'The trouble with young people today is you're all obsessed with physical perfection.' But he's already inside.

'You should chillax,' says my stepmother. 'You're pushing him away.'

An hour later, I've done the shopping and Albert climbs back into the car.

'I've been thinking…' he says.

I glance at his hair. It looks exactly the same.

'…about what you said about the changing high street reflecting the modern obsession with physical appearance.'

I narrow my eyes, scanning for bullshit. His face is wearing a familiar expression that I can't quite place – eyebrows raised, lips pulled into a smile that could well be a sneer.

'On one level, what you said is like… true, but on another level it's, like…, simplistic.

Think about it.'

'I'm thinking,' I say, my synapses and neurones sparking into action, trying to work out where I've seen that expression before.

'People buy bread, veg, meat, online, but they can't get tattooed online or get their nails painted or top up their tan, not without being there. North Parade hasn't changed *just* because of the modern-day obsession with…' He draws speech tags in the air before saying, 'preening.'

And suddenly, I place it. His expression. It's mine. The one I used to shoot at my stepmother when I'd out-clevered her. The smart-arse look that said, I'm going somewhere to be somebody and when I do, I'll never look back.

It hits me like a slap as the morning replays itself and I see my own scorn, not Albert's – my own generalisations, my own words spoken in my stepmother's voice, in our shared voice, and I realise I'm holding onto the worst of her – to soften the loss… to soften the grief.

I start the engine and catch my eyes welling up as I look into the rear-view mirror.

'You know I always loved you, don't you?'

The words echo round the car as I pull away. I'm not entirely sure who said them.

'Mum?' I think.

But my stepmother says nothing because she's been dead for eleven weeks and three days, and Albert, throwing me a what-you-on-about look, says, 'I know, Mum, and I love you too.'

27) Time, Numbers and Other Emotionally Charged Sequential Progressions

4
He ripped off the wrapping with wild excitement, threw himself at me with wide-open arms. 'Mummy,' he squealed, brim-full of everything. 'Mummy, Mummy, a puddle to paddle in.'

4+5
The austringer handed him a battered gauntlet, way too big for still-little fingers. Stiff and straight-armed, he watched the falcon land, it's talons shards of brave new moon, then turned to me and we shared the moment.

4+5+9
Then it's today and he's fixing L-plates, flying into the driving seat with Bryn as wingman now. I'm hovering on the pavement as he pulls away. Clutch. First gear. Biting point.

28) Absences I Didn't Think I'd Miss when Albert Went to Uni

1. The stroppy banter.
2. Sodden towels on the bathroom floor.
3. The so-gay-I-can't-sit-up-straight scatter cushion that's left occasional hot-pink sparkles on my oatmeal sofa that sometimes catch the synthetic daylight cast by my reading lamp, and which shine like fragments of yesterday's laughter when I'm marking year twelve *particles and radiation* assessments.

29) Lightspeed

'I'm going to see a therapist,' says Bryn.

'Oh?' I say.

'They're offering sessions at work.'

'Okay,' I say.

'A rep from the FBU did a presentation and I thought I'd lead by example and sign up. It's meant to help you process trauma experienced in the line of duty and I reckon if I sign up Rhodri and Huw will too.'

'Great idea,' I say.

'Night then, bach.'

'Night,' I say, switching off my bedside lamp.

Over on the wall by the big bay bedroom window, moonlight reflected off the sea starts moving in waves, rippling and shimmering in delicate pattens. It's beautiful and dynamic and I think how I'd think it was witchcraft if I didn't know the science. I watch it dancing for a couple of transitory seconds until it disappears just as suddenly as it started – blocked out by a passing cloud perhaps. And that's when I decide. Just like that. I'll find a therapist too, one who'll help me make sense of the fragments of madness and tragedy that've made up my life. I close my eyes as I think it through, hoping the therapeutic talking will be as swift and effective as the conversation I just had with my husband.

30) The Trouble with Gravity

Owain. Five years old. A sunny afternoon.

Owain on a sunny afternoon dressed in emerald leggings and a sage-green tee-shirt, buzzing round the bottom patio of the steep-tiered garden. The sharp concrete steps tower up to the top patio where Bryn's planning to have a barbecue later today so long as the weather and Owain behave themselves. Owain's promised to not go near the edge of the pavement on the busy main road, or jump off the spinning roundabout down the park, or stand too close to the unpredictable waves. He runs up to the very top of the garden because if he stands on his tiptoes at the highest point, he can see a silvery glimpse of the Irish Sea, feel a cool lick of wind on his serious cheek.

Me. In the kitchen. Wrapping clingfilm round and round two wing-shaped loops of green garden wire – again and again until they become opaque and shimmery. They look so much better than I'd expected, iridescent and pinkish green like the inside of shells or real insects' wings. Bryn and Albert tumble into the kitchen in a mad dash because they're running late for the big match – Aberystwyth Town versus Newi Cefn Druids. I hold the wings up as they flash past, and they stop for a moment. I catch the amusement in Bryn's eyes.

'Best clingfilm, garden-wire greenfly wings I've ever seen, bach.' He laughs as Albert pulls him toward the front door.

Smiling out into clean white sunlight, excited to give my youngest his wings. He comes when I call, and his eyes are as wide as the sky as I bend to tie the wings in place with a shiny green ribbon I bought from Glynis's stall in the Market Hall.

'Hold still,' I chide as I tie the wings to him, tutting when a wisp of cloud scuds over the springtime sun, casting a fast-moving shadow over the moment. 'Now you won't mind, will you, if you don't win a prize? They're very good wings but they might not win.' But he doesn't hear because he's filled with amazement.

'I wasn't sure you could do it,' he chirps. 'But you really, really, *really* did.' And he buzzes around in a flurry of fun. His joy is contagious, so I dash inside to get the camera, to preserve it forever.

Owain buzzing round the steep back garden wearing his brilliant greenfly wings, climbing the steps to the very top patio, balancing on the highest lump of jagged rock, raising his chin to the wind and his arms to the sky, shouting, 'Ready…steady… FLY.'

31) Invisibility

'Cerulean sky, thistledown clouds, ice-creams bought from Don Gelato's.'

I pause and glance over at Gwen from my usual place on her leatherette therapy couch. Her short grey bob is dull like brushed steel in the subdued lamplight as she sits and listens. I close my eyes and slip back into the memory.

'We're at the beach, now,' I say. 'My dad's rattling on about how he got his scar when the head spun off the polisher at work and sliced down to the bone. Albert looks at his grandad's knee, then points to a silvery dash on his own shin. "I fell off my scooter," he says. "Landed on broken glass." Owain's quiet, licking mint-choc-chip.

Bryn rolls up his shorts.

"Two grafts," he says. "But I can't feel it now." His burn is white and taut.

"That's good," says my dad.

"Well, it is and it isn't," says Bryn, staring out to sea. "I mean, it's totally numb."

"Oh," says Dad, letting his gaze follow Bryn's to the horizon.

I pick up a pebble – plum-shaped and sun-warmed, roll it in my free hand.

"If you hadn't got burned," I say. "We'd never have met in the doctor's that day." Bryn nods and smiles, touches my hand.

"All my scars are on the inside," I say.

Owain pulls up his fringe to reveal a two-inch zigzag running from the middle of his hairline.

"This is from that time I fell down the steps in the back garden because Mum made me fancy-dress wings and I tried to fly."

I say sorry for the millionth time.

"I think it looks cool," says Bryn. "Like Harry Potter." Then he ruffles Owain's hair as everyone licks and swallows and stares out to sea. "Anyhow, how did we get onto scars? A rubbish subject for a day by the sea."

"Rubbish," snaps my stepmum. "Scars are a brilliant topic." My insides clench like they used to when I was little. I give her a "don't-start" look, but she stares through me and I feel my dander rise.

"Why?" I snap.

"Isn't it obvious?" she says, fixing me now with her granite gaze. "Scars are proof of something suffered. Invisible hurt proffers scant sympathy and therefore often goes misunderstood.'"

The emotion jolts me out of the memory and my voice cracks as I lift my head and say, 'It was as near to an apology as she ever got, you know, Gwen.'

Gwen's face is calm. 'And is that where the memory ends? Or is there anything else?'

I close my eyes. It feels so real, this recollection – sun on my face, breeze in my hair, the taste of sugar and salt when I lick my lips. I watch my stepmum turn to Owain.

"And Owain, my lad," she says.

He stops licking and listens intently – I'd forgotten how much they loved each other – how much he always listened to her.

"Scars speak of recovery too. Embrace that recovery, my darling lad, and stop blaming folks for accidents that couldn't be helped."'

32) A Personal Theory of Relativity Arrived at After a Year in Therapy

Parenthood is not necessarily limited to the people you're genetically connected to.

33) The Circular Orbit of Drones

Have you sliced the beans? Have you seasoned the meat? Have you cleaned the pan beside the bread machine?

On he rattles with his head-chef questions. He could be saying anything for all I care, or chanting the same old thing again and again, because there's nowhere to go and no one to see and nothing to do but pointless preparation on this flat and futile Sunday afternoon. Well, this sous-chef wife ain't for listening. She's drifting off, somewhere else.

By the time I've floated up to the ceiling, Bryn's words are a distant drone – meaningless consonants, hollow and empty. I gaze below me, marvelling at how different everything looks from up here – the cooker, the sink – as flat as photos. I call down to tell him, but my tongue is cold and sharp, and there's a strange metallic taste inside my mouth. I wave to get his attention and feel myself lurching sideward. That's when I realise. I'm not floating, but hovering. I process the change and recalibrate, assessing my new appendages, and am surprised to find I know all their names: a canopy to protect my motor, propellers to keep me airborne, landing skids for if I ever decide to return to earth. I focus my wireless receptors and tune into my husband.

'Have you sliced the beans? Have you seasoned the meat? Have you cleaned the pan beside the bread machine?'

I feel strangely calm because he hasn't changed, and I whizz round the lampshade to hone my skills. Why have I never noticed how high and wide the kitchen is? I drop myself into his personal airspace, spinning my blades just millimetres from his face. He doesn't look up; he carries on cooking and chopping and chanting. I'm not irritated. His sameness feels like safety, freedom even, and it gives me courage. I dart up to the half-open skylight where my sharp edges catch the sunlight, then I glide outside.

'Today is only mine,' I call in my new tinny voice, because he deserves the truth after twenty-five years of marriage. And that's when he looks up – his face all zeros, his mouth, his eyes, his upturned head, tipped back in circular surprise. I feel a pang of sadness for him, anchored as he is on the heavy earth where he's always, always been.

By suppertime I'm exhausted and buzz back home. I've travelled countryside and mountains, lakes and parks; skimmed the surface of rivers and the turbulent sea – all dull and distant like dreary maps of themselves. He's sitting, waiting at the table that's neatly laid for two. I hang over his right shoulder to decompress and he plugs me in to recharge my batteries. I can't smell his human food yet but I'm close enough to know that the beans have been sautéed very gently, that the fresh-baked bread is melting the butter, that the meat has been cooked for hours and hours until it's deliciously, achingly soft and tender.

34) Chaotic Flakes

When you storm out of the front door, slamming into the midnight fast and antsy, thinking in fragments that whizz and whistle round your mind's eye, and you're oblivious to the cold on your salty cheeks or the loud-quick clip of your staccato boots through the midwinter dark, and you walk and walk breathing sharp and jerky, past the old police station into Queen's Road until you take a long deep breath that, eventually and inevitably, cuts through the chaos, and you slow right down, frowning into the night like you've just woken up mid-sleepwalk. When you watch your breath smoke up into the starless dark, and an impossible sparkle catches your eye – a glittering speck in the air – and you lift your head to see a million mots morphing into lacy flakes, tiny galaxies swirling then landing on your outstretched hand, settling on the quiet road where they form a quick white covering, and you shiver and glance behind you, at the eerie church lit by the amber gloom of a single streetlamp, and you turn for home, teeth chattering, walking fast again, not out of anger any more – that dissolved as soon as you saw the flakes, which almost never form here down by the sea – but because the gloomy town has become full of looming shadows and weird noises, and although the fast-falling snow is muffling your footsteps so they're quieter than your heartbeat that's pounding in your head, you wish they were quieter still, and when you round that final corner, onto the seafront again into an icy blast of freezing wind, almost running because you're so glad to see the familiar bricks of home that you fairly leap up the breathless steps, fling the front door open into a wall of warmth that reddens your hot-cold face, and Bryn's stood there in the vestibule, wearing his fat salopettes and that old polar coat that's been hanging in the Narnia wardrobe since the Christmas before last when you fancied learning how to ski.

When the snowflakes in your eyelashes melt in relief as much as anything else, and you want to laugh and laugh because he looks so comical, but you don't because his expression is serious – sort of angry and relieved at the same time (he's been worried sick and was just about to go out to find you) – so you shoot him that look, the one that always melts into smiles on both your faces, and you tumble into each other's arms, and make clumsy love right there in the vestibule, numb-finger fumbling with hilarious zips, lost in the intense white magic that the snowflakes are weaving as they land wild and silent in enchanted drifts, just beyond the safety of the closed front door.

That.

35) Finality Expressed in 107 Carefully Chosen Words and Silences

Tumour. Malignant. Expect a year.

Muddled-mistaken-somebody-else's-news.

A way off yet. Time for full circles, anniversaries, birthdays. Goodbyes.

Aggressive, spreading, hope for six months.

Home assessments, hospice visits, information leaflets, kind-faced nurses, cups of tea, him sleeping eighteen hours a day, her lying awake bone-weary gazing and gazing into his face imagining cells replicating cells replicating cells replicating cells.

He was 30.

She was 22.

Together 35 years if he makes it to Easter.

Exhausted. Alone-together. Trying to make the most of this finite time. Longing to talk, but there are no more words.

36) The View from the Absolute End of the Universe

37) A Never-ending Story

Tesco's humungous – the wire shelves, the groceries – big as the ones in *Tom and Jerry*, and the shoppers are all giants. An old-lady giant walks up behind me with a basket hooked over her arm, but she doesn't see me because I'm really small and she's looking at giant apples. She accidentally catches the top of my head with her basket.

'Sorry, lovey,' she says. 'Didn't see you down there. You all right?'

I can tell by her wrinkly eyes she's a friendly giant, so I smile and nod.

'Lost your mummy?' she asks, looking behind me down the long-long aisle. I follow her gaze past the piles of fruit to columns of brightly coloured tins, all electric oranges and neon greens. Mummy's at the end by the pie counter, her face dipped in shadow looking at the packet in her hand so I can't see her features. I shake my head and point to her just as she goes round the corner. The old giant-lady smiles and says I'd better go and catch her up. I smile the same smile back and skip off, doing my special Oliver-skipping.

We went to the pictures last week to see *Oliver!* and the Artful Dodger skipped in a special way that I've been practising ever since. It's slower than ordinary skipping but miles more fun. I do it now, all the way to the pie counter. The smell gets more delicious as I go, changing from apple green to warm brown meat-and-potato pie. I turn down the aisle where Mummy just went because I want to ask her what we're having for elevenses. She's right at the bottom but near enough to hear if I call her name. I skip a bit faster, doing ordinary skips, and I'm really surprised when I don't get any closer. I skip faster again but however fast I go, she always stays exactly the same distance away. I get a lurch in my tummy like you get in a lift when you go down really fast, and when Mummy disappears round the next corner, I start to run. The next aisle's piled high with pet food, towering tall above me in tins covered with pictures of animals – massive cats and dogs that watch me as I go. Their faces change shape as I run past so their teeth start to show.

'Mummy,' I shout, tears pricking behind my wide little eyes, but she keeps on walking without looking back. 'Mummy,' I scream, running as fast as I can. 'Mummy.

Mummy. MUM. BRYN!'

And that's where I jolt awake, breathless and sweating, real tears spilling as I open my eyes, and when I do, the same old pain is sharp and raw as the first time I felt it a lifetime ago, the gut-punch knowing that I'll never see her face again. But worse than that because I've lost both my mums and my Owain's gone, and Bryn, my Bryn, is lost forever.

38) Sublimation

A month after Bryn died, two weeks since the funeral, six days after Albert flew back to the States, she stands on the top front doorstep breathing in fresh and foetid, warm sea air, waving goodbye to Huw and Rhodri. When their mini Metro vanishes round the curve of Marine Terrace, she turns back inside, oblivious to the jagged cliff edge of Constitution Hill that's been taking her breath away for decades. She *is* vaguely aware of the metallic pulse of the Irish Sea throbbing and swelling for miles and miles – but it looks like something almost alive, and she's had her fill of living things. Why couldn't they have texted or phoned instead of dropping round? Why can't people see she wants, *needs*, to be left alone? It's only when she's alone she can really *feel* him any more. By the time she's shut everything out and double-bolted the front door, she's already forgotten what they came to tell her – that the donations in lieu of flowers to the Fire Brigade Charity have reached £2,000. She trails a hand over the turned-oak banister as she floats back upstairs to the beloved chaos that's strewn, scattered, piled around the bedroom.

Albert said she should keep one thing and jettison the rest.

'His clothes aren't him, Mother,' he'd said, and, 'It's not like you're ever going to forget him.' She agrees in principle, of course she does, but it's easier said than done. He's still so present in all these things, not only metaphorically, but *actually* – in the stray hairs, particles of skin, atoms and molecules that once moved through him. There must be more atoms of him and particles of his DNA in this bedroom, she thinks, stroking his favourite cashmere sweater that's teetering on top of the 'to keep' pile, than anywhere in the known universe. She smiles as she strokes, remembering his face the day she gave it to him two Christmases ago.

'Bloody hell, Sharon, bach,' he'd said, his voice almost cross at the imagined expense, his brow furrowed with genuine surprise as he took it from last-year's reused Santa bag. She'd never bought him anything decadent in all their years together, but she'd wanted to show him she could still surprise, even after all these years. By the end of Christmas Day, he'd proper loved it – the deep emerald green, the soft caress of it against his skin.

She stops stroking and withdraws her hand, determined, this time, to keep the memories under control, selecting some safe-as-houses, ancient boxer shorts to chuck into the bin liner. For almost an hour, she does really well and it's not until she finds the beanie hat at the back of the Narnia wardrobe that a pang of grief shoots through her – and in a fragment of time shorter than the gap between heartbeats, she's already remembered – how he broke a finger rescuing that family in Clarach, how he'd whinged for weeks about how it ached, how he'd laughed out loud when she gave him the hat. She reads the curlicue letters embroidered on the front in shiny, pink thread. *Woman Up*, they spell, like a message from beyond the grave, and she grins as she pulls it onto her own head, turning to the safety of yesteryear's socks. But at the bottom of the sock drawer lurks the cream-coloured scarf with its big grey stain that no amount of washing would ever shift, and there they are – twenty years ago, laughing like drains, pissed as farts at Loch Marie, picnicking on plastic cheese and peaty Glenfiddich, spilling the whisky in a moment of passion as they made out in the rain in the sharp, gritty shingle. She distracts the grief by wrapping the scarf around her neck and sorting through his football stuff.

The bedroom's almost dark and stacked with filled bin-liners by the time she's had enough. She carries the cashmere sweater to her dressing-table drawer like she might a baby, laying a hand in flat protection over its cherished softness, too tired and spent now to block the clamouring memories that are pushing to the front of her thoughts. She hugs the sweater as she lets them in – how he wore it every day when the chemo started, how she handwashed and handwashed it so many times, drying it as fast as she could in front of the fire, how the sicker he got, the more he wanted to wear it, so she bought another, exactly the same, how he wore the twin sweater in his no-frills coffin to keep him cosy for all eternity. And suddenly it's just too much. The tears cry themselves whether she likes it or not and she presses her face into the gossamer wool, weeping, weeping, not in gentle relief, but in raging waves that rip through her. And when finally, finally, she's cried herself dry, and her head is aching as much as her heart, the jumper's damp and smeared with snot. She pulls it on over the hat and scarf, hugging it to her like she once clung to him. It's huge and baggy and reaches her knees and though it's light and fine, it's heavy with sorrow, and drags her down onto the bed. She lies on her back, pulling it up over her face to really, really breathe him in, and as she does, she feels a stirring deep inside, rising up and coming alive, and suddenly her hands are not her own, moving, hungry, urgent, firm – her fingers, his fingers, loving and sure, searching the places shared only with him. She soars up and away, gasping, breathless. And when the rapture's passed and she's damp with sweat, she breathes him out a final time and falls into a dreamless sleep.

39) Aristotle's Vacuum

This isn't my childhood home. They moved here long after I left for uni. It's the home they chose together, shared together, grew old in together. The bedroom's all white-fitted wardrobes and smells so strongly of my stepmother's pachouli perfume I think she might pop out of the en suite any minute now, even after all this time.

The Boxing Day party was in full swing when I parked the Beetle last night. Auntie Norma opened the door and I hugged and air-kissed my way through the throng and found Dad in the kitchen topping up the never-ending buffet with perpetual sausage rolls. He handed me a Cheeky Vimto and, bellowing over the top of our Alan, who was murdering 'Jolene' on the karaoke, shouted, 'I've been sorting out some bits and bobs, love. They're upstairs in the bedroom. I'll give them to you tomorrow after breakfast.'

'Fair do's,' I said. 'I'll give you this year's socks then, too.' And I took my Cheeky Vimto to join *R Alan* and Dolly for the final maudlin chorus.

We always did Christmas on Boxing Day when I was growing up because my stepmum always worked.

Christmas was the busiest day of the year down the Coronary Care Unit, what with the too-much-food-and-booze and double measures of seasonal stress. When she retired and even after she passed away, the family kept up the tradition, but the year Bryn died, Dad turned eighty-five and announced he was going to downsize and get himself a nice little flat. This year's gathering, he said, will be the last. Which is why, on the morning of a weirdly warm December 26th, I packed my grief into an overnight rucksack and dragged it with me all the way to Burnley.

Getting kalied with R Alan was something like therapy, but the next morning I was bleary-eyed and morning-after-the-night-befored. When Dad plonked an impossible full-English down in front of me, I almost retched. I took a ginger sip from my mug of tea and asked how he was doing getting ready for the big move.

'Looking forward to it,' he said, but he sat, fidgety like he couldn't quite contain the grief even after all this time. I felt closer to him than I ever had in all my life as I swallowed my own feelings with another mouthful of tea and gave him his Christmas socks. The breakfast was still untouched when we went upstairs to look through the bits and bobs.

There's an old white shoebox on the powder-blue duvet. Dad takes something from it and I shoot him a look that's an unspoken question, but he doesn't communicate in glance language like the rest of the family, so I dip my eyes to the crumpled photo – two monochrome teenagers standing in a hayfield, hand-in-hand, a million years ago. They look directly at me, smiling widely. His fifties quiff would be fashionable again today but her net underskirts situate them somewhen else. The lad looks like Albert round the eyes and the girl looks a lot like…

I don't look up. I hold on tight because suddenly I'm floating in something like that slow-motion, silent time you get after an earthquake, before the screaming starts. Must be some sort of subconscious defence mechanism. Whatever it is, I'm really grateful, because I don't want Dad to see what's happening inside my head; he's wobbly and vulnerable and doesn't need my histrionics setting him off. I stand externally firm as I look and float, and as I do, a voice starts rolling round my head, my old physics teacher's voice – Dr Sharples, saying something he always used to, something he attributed to Aristotle and was always repeating, not in relation to science necessarily, but as an antidote for empty headedness or a sort of universal truth. His voice is clear and real inside my mind. *Nature abhors a vacuum. Nature requires every space to be filled with something.* The soft northern vowels construct the words over and over as my universe shifts. Slips. Resettles. And the Mum-shaped vacuum that's always been sitting in the empty middle of me fills up, with her actual face.

40) How to Convert to Positive Energy

1. Make kindling by chopping wood along natural grain. A little axe with a string-wound handle's best. Bryn customised mine donkey's years ago for a firmer grip.
2. Place kindling into wicker basket on top of big logs, then carry basket down garden as day fades.
3. Watch brand-new, hot-pink metallic-sheen trainers crunch like apples over frosty lawn, laughing out loud, thinking how Albert must've howled when he bought them, imagining his mother doing this very task, practically but improbably shod.
4. Lay basket beside stove, already prepped – riddled empty of yesterday's ash, redbrick hearth tiles swept clean, coal bucket full. Make sure fire-window's properly clean so flames can paint walls with caramel light.
5. Make newspaper firelighters like Grandad Frank showed you lifetimes ago by rolling sheets lengthways into tight tubes. Bend in middle so

right-angled then criss-cross over and over until concertinaed. Tuck in ends and lay in grate. Five should do.

6. Place kindling on top, then two logs. Open flue for maximum draw before lighting. Watch fledgling flames start quiet and dark until circulating air draws them up to catch the kindling. When flames are fierce in roaring spikes, add coal. Watch black smoke swirl upwards, pulling gentler flames through in rich golds and coppers. When coal is properly caught, close flue to slow draw. A well-managed bucket of coal will keep the room golden way past midnight.
7. Settle back onto oatmeal sofa, releasing ghosts from photos on dark-oak sideboard. Smile at memory of your wedding day, then both your dead mothers as Albert and Owain walk past, seven and four again, to smoke-post their Santa letters up yesterday's chimney, burning them all the way to the North Pole. Watch Bryn as he steps out of 1995 wearing those awful cords he had on the day of the 24-hour power-cut when you cooked stew on the camping stove and taught the boys to play poker by candlelight. Remember how at bedtime Owain asked if you could have another power-cut tomorrow because they're so much fun. Let ghosts settle back into yesteryear.

8. Focus on latest photo. You, Albert and Fabio in New York this summer. They're suited and sophisticated on their wedding day, older than Bryn was the year you married. Think about spring when they'll visit next. At bedtime, flue fire right down and watch embers fade to grey, knowing that by morning, they'll be spent cinders. Smile. If there's one thing life has taught you, it's that making light and warmth is always worth it even if it often ends in ash.
9. Go to bed, holding onto as much of the warmth and light as you can.

41) The Mindful Time-Traveller's Guide to Quantum Entanglement – the Phenomenon Whereby Two or More Objects Behave with Reference to Each Other Even Though They May be Spatially Separated

a. Once trapped behind the forcefield, don't think about the circularity of Saturn, or the glimpses you missed, or the tragedies that linger longer the more you mind them.

b. Accept your new universe.

c. Embrace the timelessness, holding a moment, stringing it out as far as it will go.

d. Picture someone else doing the same. Somewhere, somewhen. They will be, you know. They already are.
e. Ride the aching wave of separation, feeling beyond the hollow yearning to the strangeness and charm of a very real connection.
f. Smile just slightly, imagining the someone smiling back at you.

About the Author

Jan Kaneen is a granny, mum, step-mum, wife, sister, auntie, daughter, daughter-in-law, carer and now, writer. She has an MA in Creative Writing (with distinction) from the Open University and writes as a form of therapy or exorcism – to leave overpowering emotions on the page and not in her. Her flash fictions and short stories have won prizes in places like Flash 500, National Flash Fiction Day, Molotov Cocktail, Retreat West, Segora Short Story Competition, Fountain Magazine Essay Competition,

InkTears, Bath Flash and the Ellipsis First Collection competition, and she's been nominated for a Pushcart/ Best on the Net every year since 2016. She's also been a finalist in the Cheshire Prize for Literature, Comma Press's Dinesh Allirajah Prize, the Aesthetica short fiction prize and, most recently, the inaugural Curae Prize. Her debut memoir-in-flash *The Naming of Bones* was published in 2021 by Retreat West Books.

Acknowledgements

First of all, thanks to John Brantingham who judged the 2023 Bath Novella-in-flash Award – for choosing my entry and for the supportive and positive feedback he provided. Thank you too to Jude Higgins for publishing *A Learning Curve*, and for being a beacon of the flash community. Thanks also to Jeanette Sheppard for creating the beautiful artwork for the cover and Johanna Robinson for her care and diligence proofing my words.

A Learning Curve is a found story woven together from flash fictions written over five years, some of which draw from personal experience, some of which are entirely fictional and several of which were written whilst completing an MA in Creative Writing at the Open University. My Open Uni feedback buddies were invaluable background support in the development of many of the flash fictions included here, and I'd like to thank David Artis, Sharon Boyle, Maureen Bowden, Judith Field, Ruth Guthrie, Thomas Malloch, Alli Mathew, Ali McGrane and Simon O'Mahoney for their thoughts, corrections, critiques, and encouragement. I'd also like to thank Sherry Morris and Michelle Christophorou – friends and feedback buddies and all-round brilliant, talented humans who helped me in so many ways getting my novella out into the world. I feel lucky and blessed to know you all.

Previously Published

Many thanks to the following venues where these pieces appeared, sometimes in an earlier form:

'Recipe for Disaster'– first published in Fish Winners Anthology, Fish Publishing (Jan 2020)

'What Went Through my Mind in the Lecture About the Butterfly Effect in Chaos Theory – the Phenomenon Whereby a Minute Localised Change in a Complex System can have Large Effect Elsewhere', Winner of Flash 500 Competition (Jan 2020)

'Things I Saw and Felt Whilst Balancing a Tower of Pebbles on Aberystwyth Beach the Day I Finished my Finals', published at Micro Madness (June 2022)

'The Difference Between Theory and Practice, intro, Parts 1, 2 and 3', first published as 'Voices and Monsters', at Fountain Magazine (Sept 2021)

'Unpunctuated Osmium', first published online by Reflex (June 2019) then in print in 'A Girl's Guide to Flyfishing Anthology', Reflex Press (July 2020)

'Paradoxical Voices as Evoked by Doors', first published by Micro Madness (June 2019)

'Different States of Broken', first published in Ellipsis Magazine, 'One' (2018)

'Impossibility', first published in No Bindings Magazine (Jan 2017)

'How to Fill the Unfillable Void', first published online as 'How to Keep the Hunger at Bay,' at Writers' HQ (Sept 2019)

'Albert Defining Words Just Before I Challenge his Use of Possessive Pronouns', first published at The Drabble (June 2018)

'The Difference Between Schrödinger and Albert at Weekends', first published online as 'The Difference Between my Cat and Teenage Daughter at Weekends' at Reflex (March 2021) then in print in 'Beguiled by a Wild Thing Anthology,' Reflex Press (June 2021)

'Time, Numbers and Other Emotionally Charged Sequential Progressions', first published in Flash Festival Four Anthology, Ad Hoc Fiction (March 2022)

'The Circular Orbit of Drones', first published in 'The Weight of Feathers Anthology,' Retreat West Books (Sept 2021)

'Chaotic Flakes', first published as 'Flakes', winner of the Retreat West lust-themed flash competition (Nov 2016)

'A Never-ending Story', first published online at Fictive Dream (Feb 2020)

'How to Convert to Positive Energy,' first published as 'How to Stay Warm in the Winter', in Halo Magazine (Dec 2016)

'The Mindful Time-Traveller's Guide to Quantum Entanglement – the Phenomenon Whereby Two or More Objects Behave with Reference to Each Other Even Though They May be Spatially Separated', winner of Write from the Heart Competition (Dec 2020)

Printed in Great Britain
by Amazon

36830090R00067